Arielle the
Wayward Fairy

Arielle the Wayward Fairy

Martha Cabados

authorHOUSE

AuthorHouse™
1663 Liberty Drive
Bloomington, IN 47403
www.authorhouse.com
Phone: 833-262-8899

Published by AuthorHouse 09/27/2023

ISBN: 979-8-8230-1470-0 (sc)
ISBN: 979-8-8230-1469-4 (e)

Library of Congress Control Number: 2023917504

Print information available on the last page.

Any people depicted in stock imagery provided by Getty Images are models, and such images are being used for illustrative purposes only. Certain stock imagery © Getty Images.

This book is printed on acid-free paper.

For Paisley,
My beautiful Great grand daughter

In a densely populated forest lived tiny fairies called the Starling Fairies with a filmy appearance. Most of them were good fairies willing to help anyone that may come their way; that is, all but one, Arielle.

Arielle was orphaned at a very early age, and she was hurt and angry to be left alone in the fairy world with nothing; not even a parent.

As she sat on a twig one day sobbing, a fairy Godmother approached her to console her. Being a good fairy, she helped Arielle by giving her a magic wand to take care of herself; primarily to find food and a home. However, instead of using the wand for a good purpose, she used it for power.

Within the fairy kingdom there was an intense desire to own a starling. According to the legend you would obtain everlasting life if you caught and raised one; so goes the legend.

A meeting was to be held today by Queen Rhiannon, the fairy's keeper. While Arielle was waiting for the queen to arrive, she danced among flowers and thistles in a nearby swamp.

When Queen Rhiannon arrived, all the fairies were present

to hear her advice. Once there, she approached them. She looked around at the crowd and began her speech.

"The starlings have arrived. They are roosting at the edge of the forest on the west side. It's up to each of you to catch one so you must have a method of capture and a plan for safe keeping. Starlings have always been a mystery to fairy folk. They can be taught to talk or mimic and perhaps even sing. The master of the bird is the sole keeper. The starling must be fed and watered daily to stay alive. It will be up to you to train the bird to your satisfaction if you wish him trained.

Arielle listened intently. She would catch a starling all right, but not for everlasting life. She would use it to enrich her life.

"All right every one; you are on your own. Good luck," said the queen.

A cloud of silvery dust filled the air as the fairies ascended into the air. Arielle knew exactly what she was going to do. She flew off in the opposite direction of the others to attack from behind while the others would be facing them head on.

Before she arrived at the edge of the forest, she looked for a large cobweb among the trees. She traveled quite a distance before she found the one she was looking for.

While she wandered, she had thoughts of grandeur. First, she would have a home built for herself when she had made enough money. She thought of how she would manage and how much income she could make. How would she handle the income she thought? I can't operate through a bank; that is nonsense. I'm just a fairy and most people don't believe in fairies. She would have to find another way.

Arielle became tired so she didn't catch a starling that day. She waited for the other fairies to clear the forest. She looked for a place to sleep and slept at the edge of the forest in a beautiful bed of flowers.

The next morning she was awakened by a beautiful maiden working among the flowers. Frightened, she flew to a different flower. The maiden saw her when she flew.

"Oh, my goodness what a beautiful fairy; please don't be alarmed; I won't hurt you."

"Oh, uh, my name is Arielle. I live in the Eagle's Wood Forest," she said as she pointed to the forest. Where do you live?"

Ginger smiled. "I live here, Arielle. This is my garden. You are the first fairy I've ever seen and I am so blessed for that privilege. My, you are so tiny," said Ginger.

Arielle laughed and it sounded like bells tinkling. "Fairy folk are tiny, Ginger."

She flew up to Ginger's shoulder and Ginger walked to the garden table and set down on a bright red chair. They talked until noon and became new friends.

After their chat, Arielle left her company and entered the forest to look for a starling. She first looked for a large web. After it was found, she went deeper into the forest to find a large male starling. He needed to be big and strong to carry her and the coins she would be taking.

As she looked, she spotted Clover, a fairy she didn't like or trust.

"Hi, Arielle," greeted Clover.

"Are you following me again nosey britches?" asked Arielle.

"No, no, I. ..."

Because Arielle didn't believe her, she slapped the spider web over her and took her to a tall tree, and placed her at the end of a sturdy branch.

"Arielle, stop it," shrieked Clover "Get me out of here."

Arielle slipped her wand from her pocket and wound Clover tighter.

"Stop, stop, Arielle." she screamed. A spider is coming Arielle, please help me," she shrieked.

Arielle watched the spider and listened to Clover scream. "Are you going to stop following me and calling me names?" she asked Clover.

"Yes, yes, please get me out of here, Arielle."

"Okay, Miss Goody-Two-Shoes but don't you dare tell a soul about this or the next time I won't let you go."

Just as the spider was going to attack Clover, Arielle zapped it with her wand and watched it fall to the ground. She continued through the forest but now she had to look for another web to catch a starling. Once she found one to her liking, she searched for a male starling. She flew until she spotted a large healthy one then she tossed the web over him. Immediately he began screeching.

"Now, now, don't get excited. You and I are going to be very good friends. You may as well get used to the idea. I am your master now and I will train you to do my bidding," said Arielle. She carefully tucked the web around him while he squawked angrily. She picked the bird up and carried him to her home in a hollow tree in the forest. Inside the oak she had a cage that she had taken from a house in a distant village for the birds' safekeeping. She opened the door and placed him inside.

Bright and early the next morning Arielle went to the bird's cage. She was anxious to start his training. "Good morning, friend," she said. "This is your new home; how do you like it? Uhhh, I think we'll call you Magic because that is what you're going to be, like a magic carpet. I'm going to teach you to yield to my orders, Magic. We will become as one."

"Caw, caw, caw," the bird squawked. Arielle squinted at him. "You're not a crow, why are you acting like one?"

"Bob White, bob white," squawked the bird again.

"My goodness, Magic, what a fancy talker you are; and such a good boy. I think you'll be very easy to train." She wanted him to understand her instructions and also be a good companion.

While training Magic, Arielle became his trusted friend and he became hers as well. When Arielle was satisfied with the training, she opened the cage door.

Magic jumped up and down screeching, "Yay, yay, yay!"

Arielle laughed. "You like being free, Magic?"

"Free. Good boy, good boy."

Arielle laughed again and said, "You certainly are Magic, and what a good job you've done."

"Good job, good job."

Arielle smiled as she set him on the floor inside her home in the oak tree.

"I'm going to fly onto your back, Magic, don't be alarmed."

"Okay, okay, no alarm," said Magic.

Arielle smiled and flew onto his back then stroked his feathers. "You are such a good boy."

"Good boy, Magic."

"Let's fly, North, Northeast, Magic."

Magic obeyed and they ascended into the sky. Arielle let him fly for a while to give him exercise since he had been cooped up so long.

"Let's go home now, Magic. You've done so well today. Tomorrow we'll visit my friend, Ginger. She is a human and is going to help us with our project. She's very pretty Magic, with long flowing blond hair. I met her in her garden among the flowers. She will be so proud of you."

"Ginger proud."

"Yes, I want the two of you to become friends. In the near future, we'll be taking some very long trips. I want you to exercise to gain strength."

"Become friends, Ginger," said Magic.

Ginger is Arielle's cover. If Ginger is doing the banking and hires contractors to build the mansion for Arielle; no one, including the queen, is going to suspect her of stealing from the tooth fairies.

The next day Arielle stepped outside and spotted Clover. She reached into a pocket for her wand but Clover saw her and quickly jumped behind a tree.

"Clover, you said you wouldn't call me anymore names or follow me. You'd better think your actions over again."

Clover peeked out from behind the tree. "I haven't called you any names, Arielle, and I didn't promise you anything else. I can go where I want; do what I want, anytime I want and you can't stop me."

"We will see about that, Clover. Just watch your step."

Two weeks later, Arielle and Magic left on their first journey. It is to be a flight of hope for Arielle. She has one thing to accomplish over the next year and that is to have a beautiful home built for herself, Magic and Ginger.

When they arrived in Beaver Falls, Arielle gave Magic instructions. "Stop here, Magic."

"Where Master?"

"Down there at the big brown house," she said as she pointed. "Little Jimmy's house first," said Arielle.

Magic swooped down to the porch. Arielle found an entry and was inside within minutes. At Jimmy's bed, she slipped the coins from under his pillow and disappeared into the night.

"Money tonight, Master?"

"Oh yes, Magic. The tooth fairy was very generous. Let's go across the street to Jessica's house."

Magic soared down to the veranda. Arielle slipped through an open window and sneaked into the bedroom to Jessica's bed and took the money from under her pillow. Arielle tossed the coins into her money bag and hurried back to Magic. They stopped at house after house until the bag is so heavy it was hard for Arielle to carry.

"Home now, Master?"

"Why Magic! I do believe you're reading my mind. We will stop at Ginger's first to deliver the money and tomorrow we will collect more."

"Good. Need more money."

Arielle laughed. "Yes, Magic, lots of money for our mansion. Ginger is keeping track of it, and she will take it to the bank and deposit it. She will let us know when we have enough to start building."

Word spread throughout the human population that someone was taking money from under the pillows of the children. The townspeople begin locking their doors and barring their windows.

Two weeks later Arielle and Magic made another trip.

"Where to go tonight, Master?"

"Let's head over to the village in Beaver Falls again, Magic."

When they arrived at one of the homes, Arielle tried every window in the house. She pulled, tugged, and pushed but the windows wouldn't budge. She stood back with her hands on her hips and looked at Magic with a peeved expression.

"Locked?" asked Magic.

"Yes, Magic, this is a job for you. Go down through the chimney and take the money from under Kaden's pillow."

Magic did what Arielle asked and returned to her with the money in his beak and dropped it into her money bag. "Good job, Master? I'm no Santa Claus, for sure."

Arielle let out a peal of laughter. Magic shook to release the soot on his feathers then looked at his Master. She is covered head to toe in black soot. Magic roared with laughter.

"Wh-What, Magic? Why are you laughing?"

"You should see, Master. A beautiful fairy turned wicked witch."

"That's not funny Magic but you've done a very good job. There is more than one way to outfox these humans. They aren't going to interfere with my plans. I have the power and the knowledge, and I will use them to my advantage." She and Magic continue their journeys as her wealth builds.

Queen Rhiannon heard the whispering of a thief in the night and talk of Arielle's long trips. A meeting is called the next day for all fairies under Old Noble. "I've heard whispers of someone stealing money from children that was left by our tooth fairies. Arielle, I hear you have been taking long trips." said Queen Rhiannon giving her a distasteful look.

"Oh no, it's not me, Your Highness. I would never do anything like that; but I do take long trips when I take Magic out for exercise." Arielle crossed her fingers behind her back; she was not about to admit to her money-making plan, not now, not ever.

"If anyone of you is caught stealing, you'll be severely punished. We must be do-good fairies to survive over the ages and to protect our reputation," said Queen Rhiannon.

Arielle glanced over and saw Clover but also saw a male fairy looking at her. She became uncomfortable but ignored him. After the meeting, Arielle flew home and fed Magic.

"Magic, we'll travel a few more days then we must take a break.

After our break we will go to the villages and banish every wish that was wished upon a star. What do think about that, Magic?"

"Yeah, yeah, yeah, banish wishes."

"After that, we'll undo every good deed that the Fairy Godmother's have done, agreed, Magic?"

"Yeah, yeah, yeah, agreed."

"Magic, you're actually learning to agree with me." Arielle laughed happily.

Tomorrow a banquet for the Queen is being held beneath Old Noble. The Queen is leaving the forest for other obligations. The banquet is a happy occasion for all fairies. While at the celebration, Clover approached Arielle.

"Arielle, I'd like you to meet my friend, Naida. She also has special powers like you but unlike you; she is a servant of the queen. I know you're the one taking money from children, Arielle, but I have no proof and until I do, I'll be watching every move you make."

Arielle ignored Clover and turned to Naida. "It is nice meeting you Naida," said Arielle thinking now she has two spies working against her instead of one. She looked back at Clover and said, "Gee Clover, maybe I should have let that spider eat you. You haven't changed a bit."

Naida looked at Arielle with questioning eyes. Arielle held her tongue from further remarks but knew that Clover had something up her sleeve again.

After Queen Rhiannon left, Arielle planned to take the wishes made upon a star to a far-off land. She came up with a chant that would work. By dusk the following day she was ready for her trip. She went to Magic's cage and freed him and flew onto his back.

"Going where Master?"

"We'll be going to Bay Village tonight, Magic, we have a big job to do but first I must summon the fireflies." Arielle circled her wand as she chanted. "Fireflies of the night; come with me on our flight. Any wish upon a star will be strewed to lands afar."

Thousands of fireflies followed her into the night. They resembled flickering torches of marching soldiers.

"Awesome, Master, awesome, beautiful."

Unknown to Arielle, Clover and Naida had been watching from behind another tree and followed them.

When Arielle and Magic arrived in the village, she began chanting as she circled her wand and repeated the chants over and over until the fireflies had gathered all the wishes.

Once they began their trip, the fireflies suddenly turned back. Arielle looked around and was shocked at their behavior. They were flying up and down, in circles and from side to side like they were confused.

"Something wrong, Master?"

"I'm not sure, Magic, they are acting strange."

Below, Clover and Naida have their sights on the fireflies. Naida had held up her wand and was chanting. "Fireflies turn your flight; good versus evil makes you right," chanted Naida.

Arielle spun around and surprisingly spotted Naida with her wand. She looked past Naida and saw Clover.

"What to do, Master?"

"Over there, Magic! There's Naida and Clover. Fly me to them, quick! I must take Naida's wand to make her powerless. They're trying to reverse my chants. Barnstorm Naida now!"

Magic flew as fast as he could toward Naida. When she saw him coming, she tried to fly away but she was no match for him. He bumped her and she dropped her wand into a pond below.

"Magic do good, Master?"

"You sure did, now let's try the chant again. Fireflies of the night; come with me on this flight; any wish upon a star, strew them out to lands afar."

The fireflies gathered the wishes again and took them to a land far away. Arielle watched the twinkling lights of the fireflies with great anticipation as they carried the wishes away.

"Go home now, Master?"

"Yes, Magic, now we can go home."

"We go tomorrow, Master?"

"Yes, since the queen has left, we're going to make money in the villages again from the tooth fairies. We'll have to keep an eye out for Naida and Clover because they may try to put a crimp in our plans again," said Arielle. "We almost have enough to start building our mansion near the forest."

"Good job, Master."

That night and every night thereafter, Arielle and Magic flew into different villages taking coins from under the children's pillows. When she had enough saved to build the mansion, Ginger approached her.

"Arielle, we have enough money to start hiring men to build your mansion," said Ginger.

"Great, can you hire a contractor tomorrow? They have to be the best and I want a huge aviary for Magic and his mate. I'd like for the mansion to have three floors near the edge of the forest with a garden on the roof for me with a lot of bluebells."

"A mate for Magic?" asked Ginger.

"Yes, when the Annual Starling Hunt begins this year, I'm going to find Magic a lady friend."

"I want you to oversee the contractors work, Ginger, and I want the aviary under the roof with a lot of bluebells and open to the world."

"Okay, Arielle, I'll do everything I can do. Oh, why bluebells, Arielle?" asked Ginger.

"They tinkle when I dance. I love them and I love bubbles too, all fairies love bluebells and bubbles," said Arielle.

"Bubbles?" asked Ginger.

"Oh, yes, they have an array of every color in the rainbow until they burst."

And so, it was. Ginger started hiring well-known contractors and she oversaw the construction, making sure everything is done right. One day Clover flew over to the new house.

"Hi, Ginger. What's going on?" asked Clover.

"It's a new building, can't you tell?"

"I know it's a building, but what kind? It looks like it's going to be huge."

"You'll find out soon enough, Clover."

history. We hope that others will be able to read our story, literally and figuratively, knowing that God can deliver you from any situation. It also allows you to put your story in a book or text that you can begin to share with our communities and family members.

Not only can your story inspire others, but it can also inspire you too! Think about it; we all have moments in our lives where we can reflect and feel motivated and inspired. On reflection, we are able to see clearly what is going well and what is challenging. You can learn from your mistakes and avoid repeating the original mistakes. Your story is also necessary so your family can see you grow as you deal with difficult situations. Your story should demonstrate your perseverance and development as a Christian.

Your story teaches others. The world will continue to evolve and change. As a Christian, it is your opportunity to assist with change, to help with change, and to grow with change. Change is difficult, but it's necessary. Allow your story to be authentic through fear, uncertainty, and exhaustion. Your honesty will help others know that you are human. It will allow them to realize that they are still human even though they have experienced pain and trauma. We need your story. Your story is necessary. It's a guide to help others navigate through situations with a positive guide by the Holy Spirit.

My story is meant to hopefully show you perseverance, steadfastness, and always being filled in the work of the Lord. Remember, you have to remember where you came from and you have to look into your past but not stay there. Therefore, it is important that you keep trying in the face of adversity. Suffering is a normal part of life. This is not an illusion. It's a sad everyday reality. From a cold to terminal cancer or from losing our keys to the bereavement of a loved one, we all face hardships in life in all its forms. What is suffering? Pain comes to us in two main ways—losing what you have (things you like are taken from you) or losing what you want. Like I said, we all face pain in different forms in our lives.

The question is how are we going to get through this? How will we meet Him? How can we endure suffering with peace of mind? We want to answer these questions. No matter where you live today, we all need to be reminded of these truths. Live to weather life's storms? How you handle the adversities you face in life then has a lot to do with how you view God. This passage teaches us that God helps us to endure suffering—divine suffering and divine sovereignty, "Who has believed [confidently trusted in, relied on, and adhered to] our message [of salvation]? And to whom [if not us] has the arm and infinite power of the Lord been revealed? For He [the Servant of God] grew up before Him like a tender shoot [plant], And like a root out of dry ground; He has no stately form or majestic splendor That we would look at Him, Nor [handsome] appearance that we would be attracted to Him. He was despised and rejected by men, A Man of sorrows and pain and acquainted with grief; And like One from whom men hide their faces He was despised, and we did not appreciate His worth or esteem Him. But [in fact] He has borne our griefs, And He has carried our sorrows and pains; Yet we [ignorantly] assumed that He was stricken, Struck down by God and degraded and humiliated [by Him]" (Isaiah 53:1–4).

Tragedy provides an opportunity to see God bring good out of every situation The psalmist King David says, "It is good for me that I have been afflicted, That I may learn Your statutes" (Psalm 119:71). Well, he's not out of balance mentally or emotionally. He doesn't say his sufferings are pleasurable when they arise. I don't even think he said that; in retrospect, he's glad they got to act. But at least that's what he said. Since they happened, he thanked God, and by his grace, he was able to get some good things out of them. The wonderful truth is that God can bring some good out of any tragedy, regardless of its nature or cause—including those caused by our own bad choices or those of others.

You might say, "Well, that might be a good rule of thumb, applicable as a general principle, but you know nothing about the tragedy I'm dealing with and its horrific complexity. Yes, even how dirty it is!" I probably don't know, that's really beside the point. The point is that God knows; God knows every tragedy in your life and mine. Paul declared in Romans 8:28, "And we know [with great confidence] that God [who is deeply concerned about us] causes all things to work together [as a plan] for good for those who love God, to those who are called according to His plan and purpose." This promise is for those who actively respond to God's call, redemption. In other words, it is a promise to those who have repented of their sins and committed themselves by faith in Jesus Christ and accepted Him as their personal Lord and Savior. Making this commitment ignites a person's love for the Savior.

When you're entering a new chapter in your life, God will miraculously bring good even out of a bad situation or a bad chapter in your life. When you're entering a new chapter in your life, "It is the Lord who goes before you; He will be with you. He will not fail you or abandon you. Do not fear or be dismayed" (Deuteronomy 31:8).

When Israel arrived at the Promised Land, they sent out twelve spies and two of them came to give a very good report on the land, but the other ten of the spies were fearful and gave a bad report because they were dismayed at the inhabitants. Their fear was highly contagious and caused the nation to not cross over and take it.

If you've ever had to move to a different city or state, you probably know something about that feeling. Even though your circumstances are different, the basic principle of God being with you is even better. "Lord ... Walking Ahead of You" should give you more peace of mind about this new chapter in your life. Consider this, He already knows the future and has *snipped* into what is happening in due course. As you browse through my story and see where I draw strength, be inspired to know that perhaps a Bible verse can give you some comfort, confidence, and assurance that God is with you as you step into a new chapter of your life. Wherever you go, you go, but as we have read, He is also before you, never forsaking or forsaking you. That's right, isn't it?

CHAPTER 3

OBEDIENCE THROUGH DEATH

G od's life-changing Word is full of promises of true love, forgiveness, redemption, peace, hope, and joy for all who put their trust in His son, Jesus. Many passages in the Bible encourage me to trust in God's abiding presence and power. The next chapter of my life will change my life, and when you read this book, you will see God's goodness and mercy. "Have I not commanded you? Be strong and courageous! Do not be terrified or dismayed [intimidated], for the Lord your God is with you wherever you go" (Joshua 1:9). "Even though I walk through the [sunless] valley of the shadow of death, I fear no evil, for You are with me; Your rod [to protect] and Your staff [to guide], they comfort and console me" (Psalm 23:4).

Dedicated to Serve God

Romans 12:1–2 says, "Therefore I urge you, brothers and sisters, by the mercies of God, to present your bodies [dedicating all of yourselves, set apart] as a living sacrifice, holy and well-pleasing to God, which is your rational [logical, intelligent] act of worship. And do not be conformed to this world [any longer with its superficial values and customs], but be transformed and progressively changed [as you mature spiritually] by the renewing of your mind [focusing on godly values and ethical attitudes], so that you may prove [for yourselves] what the will of God is, that which is good and acceptable and perfect [in His plan and purpose for you]."

Nothing matures us more than a trusting response to a redeeming God in times of tribulation. God can redeem us from the pain of life and make us more like Jesus. Looking back on my life, I can say that I have learned more from failures than from successes. I grew up in pain more than in wealth. In Romans 8:28, the writer Paul lets us know there are many things in life that can make us mature enough to endure anything, and even the most tragic and painful things in our lives should make us more like Jesus.

The death of my sibling made me want to be closer to God. He turned the arrow of the enemy, destined to destroy me, into the scalpel of the great physician, destined to heal me. God gave me a promise, "If you obey the Bible, God will do anything but fail. If you obey God, He will satisfy the desire of your heart as long as you walk uprightly beforehand." The Bible declares, "Now faith is the assurance [title deed, confirmation] of things hoped for [divinely guaranteed], and the evidence of things not seen [the conviction of their reality—faith comprehends as fact what cannot be experienced by the physical senses]" (Hebrews 11:1).

My life tells a story. I now accept this story because I have grown spiritually, and many of my experiences have led me to my destiny as a Christian leader. A lot of the things I'm passionate about today reveal a lot about me. I love helping others and seeing them experience joy, peace, love, and redemption. God promised me that He would be there for every challenge. It is the Father's desire to take us to a state of perfection in the Holy Spirit where we can transition from the natural to the supernatural. God wants you to walk in the supernatural. By faith, we have a relationship with God in Christ through the Holy Spirit. Faith unites us to Him. Faith finds strength in trials and temptations. "Therefore, since we have been justified [that is, acquitted of sin, declared blameless before God] by faith, [let us grasp the fact that] we have peace with God [and the joy of reconciliation with Him] through our Lord Jesus Christ [the Messiah, the Anointed]" (Romans 5:1).

We must consciously cultivate our faith and refuse to feed on past doubts and pain. The Lord has revealed it to me. Go forward and don't look back. The past is behind you and your future awaits you. Seize each moment and rely on God's strength, courage, and wisdom to get through this process. God will be your shield. You won't stand alone and face the world alone because whether you know God or not, He is with you. The Lord will supernaturally empower you to rise up and go forward in His strength and power. "Then he said to me, "This [continuous supply of oil] is the word of the Lord to Zerubbabel [prince of Judah], saying, 'Not by might, nor by power, but by My Spirit [of whom the oil is a symbol],' says the Lord of hosts" (Zechariah 4:6).

Why do I need obedience to commit my life to God? When I searched the scriptures and studied 1 Samuel 15, Saul chose to keep the Amalek king Agag alive and take the spoils instead of destroying everything as God commanded. When Samuel questioned him, Saul said: "I have obeyed the voice of the Lord, and have gone on the mission on which the Lord sent me, and have brought back Agag the king of Amalek, and have completely destroyed the Amalekites. But the people took some of the spoil, sheep and oxen, the best of the things [that were] to be totally destroyed, to sacrifice to the Lord your God at Gilgal" (1 Samuel 15:20–21).

Samuel answered in 1 Samuel 15:22, "Has the Lord as great a delight in burnt offerings and sacrifices. As in obedience to the voice of the Lord? Behold, to obey is better than sacrifice, And to heed [is better] than the fat of rams." Why is obedience better than sacrifice?

Two answers are given. The first answer is offered in Samuel's response, "For rebellion is as [serious as] the sin of divination [fortune-telling], And disobedience is as [serious as] false religion and idolatry. Because you have rejected the word of the Lord, He also has rejected you as king" (1 Samuel 15:23).

Saul's rebellion was an act of rebellion, injustice [sin], and idolatry.

The second answer appears in Saul's confessions. He says, "I have sinned; for I have transgressed the command of the Lord and your words, because I feared the people and obeyed their voice" (1 Samuel 15:24). Saul admitted that his sacrifice was a transgression [a sin] and a disobedience to God's command. It's a result of seeking people's approval.

As we have seen, there are several reasons why obedience to God is better than offering sacrifices or offerings to him: (1) disobedience is an act of rebellion, (2) disobedience is sin, (3) disobedience is idolatry, (4) disobedience is a disregard for God's Word, and (5) disobedience is based on goodwill toward others, not God. Even today, when we humans try to be good at serving God, there is still the temptation to perform certain religious duties instead of actually obeying God. Even good activities, such as giving money to charity, going to church, or praying in public are not as important to God as keeping His commandments.

Obedience Accompanies Faith

Hebrews 11:6–8 says, "But without faith it is impossible to [walk with God and] please Him, for whoever comes [near] to God must [necessarily] believe that God exists and that He rewards those who [earnestly and diligently] seek Him. By faith [with confidence in God and His word] Noah, being warned by God about events not yet seen, in reverence prepared an ark for the salvation of his family. By this [act of obedience] he condemned the world and became an heir of the righteousness which comes by faith. By faith Abraham, when he was called [by God], obeyed by going to a place which he was to receive as an inheritance; and he went, not knowing where he was going."

We submit when we respond to Christ. We come to the act of redemption. In the salvation event, we come "according to the foreknowledge of God the Father by the sanctifying work of the Spirit to be obedient to Jesus Christ and to be sprinkled with His blood" (1 Peter 1:2).

As Peter said, our future life is a life of obedience, "[Live] as obedient children [of God]; do not be conformed to the evil desires which governed you in your ignorance [before you knew the requirements and transforming power of the good news regarding salvation]" (1 Peter 1:14). "Since by your obedience to the truth you have purified yourselves for a sincere love of the believers, [see that you] love one another from the heart [always unselfishly seeking the best for one another]" (1 Peter 1:22).

Reward for Obedience

Obedience shows God that we love Him and trust Him, which in turn activates His power in our lives, but most importantly, obedience pays off.

Success

Everyone wants to be successful in what they do, proving that some of the best-selling books in the modern world are the ones that talk about success. Interestingly, in His word, God has given us a simple secret to success, which is to read and obey His word God has a plan for each of us—a plan to prosper us and a plan to give us a future (refer to Jeremiah 29:11). God's will for our lives is that we must succeed. Success is not defined by the world but by God; it means achieving what we were born to do. God never created us to fail or just be mediocre. God created us to be excellent. But we must align ourselves with God's will so that God's plan will be reflected in our lives. You will always be above and never below if you pay attention and earnestly obey the commandments God has given. "This Book of the Law shall not depart from your mouth, but you shall read [and meditate on] it day and night, so that you may be careful to do [everything] in accordance with all that is written in it; for then you will make your way prosperous, and then you will be successful" (Joshua 1:8).

CHAPTER 4

THE POWER OF PAIN

The power of pain is something everyone experiences, and we all deal with it in different ways. It connects us and unites us, but above all, it centers us. Remember that pain can be subconscious. Anyone who is in pain doesn't always hurt you. One thing I've realized is that pain is the universal language. This is something we all have to deal with. Pain connects us at times, but most of all, it keeps us focused where we realize that a story is often more painful within the journey than after. When I went through the most traumatic experience of my life, it was losing my mother, my best friend, and my queen. The pain I felt was indescribable. Sometimes I laugh. Sometimes I cry. Most importantly, I have many fond memories of our relationship.

I had found myself in a silent depression over the past

few months and years despite being a great woman of faith. I couldn't fathom why so many of my loved ones died within five months. However, I know my journey is in the hands of Almighty God. He made sure I was steadfast. Relying on one of my favorite scriptures to keep me grounded and grounded is Isaiah 40:31, "But those who wait for the LORD [who expect, look for, and hope in Him] Will gain new strength and renew their power; They will lift up their wings [and rise close to God] like eagles [rising toward the sun]; They will run and not become weary, They will walk and not grow tired."

One thing is clear to me we don't just suffer for ourselves. We suffer for others, and once we have had some particularly traumatic, painful experiences, we are anointed to see others through their own similar stories. It gives us authority. We now live to talk to others when they grow weary and hopeless. In this journey, we must always be aware that our past can make our present more powerful.

As I reflect on my childhood, I embraced and invited my childhood passions to guide my adult goals. What I loved as a child revealed a lot about who I was and how I am not perfect today, but those experiences shaped me and shaped my destiny today. A difficult childhood can blind you to the wonderful strengths, weaknesses, and talents you possess. During my childhood, I had to let go or hide some very important parts of myself like sensitivity, openness, and desire to succeed in my career because they might not have been understood or welcomed in my family structure.

Over the years I've worked hard to rediscover or find for the first time the things that bring you joy, peace, and laughter, so it's been worth the effort. One summer was the best as my aunt took me to upstate New Jersey away from it all, giving me the life fit for a kid from an urban New York neighborhood where drugs, single-family homes, domestic violence, homicide, and suicide could be found. Learning to take care of your own needs, finding self-compassion, loving yourself, and discovering your worth are invaluable today.

When I started going through the grieving process, it became overwhelming. Why is this happening to me? I start negotiating with God. As we all know, it is not uncommon for grieving people to feel angry and frustrated, and somehow they are trying to hold someone accountable for this great loss, but when God began to reveal to me a familiar scripture. Ecclesiastes 3:1–8 says, "To everything there is a season a time to every purpose under heaven a time to be born and a time to die, a time to plant and a time to pluck up that which is planted, a time to kill, a time to heal. a time to break down, a time to build up a time, to weep and a time to laugh, a time to mourn and a time to dance, a time to cast away stones and a time to gather stones, a time to embrace and a time to refrain from embracing, a time to get and a time to lose, a time to keep and a time to cast away, a time to rend and a time to sew, a time to keep silent and a time to speak, a time to love and a time to hate, a time of war and a time of peace."

The seven stages of processing grief are denial, anger, bargaining, depression, shock, pain and guilt, and acceptance. Denial is usually the most emotional stage. When I go through a loss, it's clear that my underlying feelings of shock and disbelief are becoming real. The physical symptoms show up as a sickness. It caused a loss of appetite, and basically, I was emotionally numb. Before long, the pain and guilt of living in the dust without my mother became unbearable. Over the years my mother had been concerned about my safety which made me feel guilty, and I immediately started having a lot of regrets. It became very difficult to deal with. As I go through the grieving process, I realize that nothing can stop loss. My depression lasted for several months and then developed into several years. My spiritual walk with God is starting to grow. I'm using my Christianity as a way to escape pain, so through my conversion, I'm attending church several times a week.

I began to feel and experience an upward movement

when I thought nothing could relieve the terrible pain. I began to see a little light at the end of the tunnel, and as I began my journey with the Lord, I felt better every day. As I matured and grew, I realized that grieving is a process. God has rebuilt my life. As the months passed and I began to come to terms with the loss, God gave me the strength to go through the grieving process. I get a lot of support from my husband who keeps encouraging me that my mom wants me to move on, and he always reassures me that patience comes with the process and to not stress myself out with the expectation that I have to accept the pain I have been through.

As I processed my pain, I found a lot of comfort in the Word of God. Isaiah 43:2–6 states, "When you pass through the waters I will be with you and through the rivers they shall not overwhelm you when you walk through the fire you will not be scorched nor will the flame burn you for I am the Lord your God the Holy One of Israel your savior. I've given Egypt to the Babylonians as your ransom and Sheba it's Providence in exchange for you because you are precious in my sight. You are honored and I love you I will give other men in return for you other people in exchange for your life. Do not fear for I am with you. I will bring your offspring from the East where they are scattered and gather you from the West, I will say to the north give them up and to the South do not hold them

29

back. Bring my son's from bar way and my daughters from the ends of the Earth."

Pain has a language of its own, the emotions and testing. Suddenly I lost my brother to murder, and the emotions and the circumstances around it put me in the worst mental space I've ever been in my life. That one event triggered a lot in different areas from knowing how to handle grief, not knowing what it looked like and what I was experiencing to the rigor of it. There was a moment when I had to snap out of it and commit to thinking and working hard and being strong. The truth is I did not want to. I did not feel like it, so I focused only on gaining energy to continue in my spiritual walk with God.

I've been through some tough times in my life, and I ask the same questions every time I fight, why me? How long does this take? What it will teach me? Life is known for testing us and then teaching us. This is the opposite of what we were taught in school. I've been taking exams my whole life, and I'm sure you have too. I think that's the way it is. During my years on Earth, I learned some valuable lessons, and one of them really resonated, turning pain into meaning! If you have to go through it, at least you get some. In every fight, there is a lesson. Ever wondered why it happened to you? I know it sounds unfair, but the truth is it happens to you because you can handle it. Life happens to all of us, but there is a part of it that is meant to empower, not kill. Remember all the times you didn't see a way out but succeeded anyway. If it happened to your best friend, it could kill him. If it happens to your enemy, it will still damage you. Your problems will be on your plate because you can swallow them.

CHAPTER 5

UNDERSTANDING THE IMPACT OF TRAUMA AND RELYING ON SPIRITUAL STRENGTH

The trauma I suffered involved a broad understanding of traumatic stress responses and the common responses I started having. Many survivors of multiple deaths may be confronted immediately or long after a traumatic experience.

While my traumatic stress response was a normal response to abnormal situations, my responses related to the trauma I experienced became intrusive memories. These included unnecessarily painful memories of traumatic events, especially murders, traumatic events as if they will

33

happen again (flashbacks), car backfiring, police sirens in urban neighborhoods, loud arguments in public, etc.

Many people process the death of an important person in their lives in different ways. One of the most common ways Americans deal with the death of a loved one is by turning to religion, which can have positive consequences. Some studies have found that coping through religious beliefs can lead to greater stress, especially when dealing with the death of a family member by homicide. My connection with God has played a big part in my recovery. I developed a positive, religious coping style that was correlated with stress-related growth, positive religious outcomes, and a developed sense of meaning.

Depression, traumatic stress, and separation stress rear themselves and expect your reaction. In addition, the connection with God is and becomes more evident. However, one of the questions I ask myself most often is "Why did God allow a tragic experience to happen to my family?" It is basically a relational question, not a theological one. It's important to consider that this question seeks why a loving God can allow anything other than love to be experienced.

I found that the best thing I could do was to recognize the profound hurt and struggle that lies within all of us who have ever wrestled with the question, "Why?" We see how Paul dealt with the unresolved struggles in his own life when he states, "Due to the transcendent greatness and extraordinariness of [revelation received from God], I, a satanic messenger, was given a thorn in my flesh for which I did not consider myself important, tormented and harassed me - so that I can't get up! For this reason I begged the Lord three times to leave me; but he said to me, "My grace is sufficient for you. For this reason I begged the Lord three times to leave me; but he said to me: "My grace is sufficient for thee [my love and mercy are more than sufficient - always available - whatever the case may be]; for [my] power Be perfect in [thy] weakness [and be perfect and express it most effectively]. Therefore, I rejoice in weakness, in insult, in affliction, in persecution, in difficulty, for Christ's sake; for when I [in When I am weak in strength] I will be strong [truly mighty, truly mighty, truly drawn from the strength of God]" (2 Corinthians 12:7–10).

After years of processing, reflection, and prayer, I can now see that God is able to express strength through my weaknesses and build a stronger character in me through some of the traumatic experiences I have gone through. I think many who read this can also see that God has built a specific strength or determination in areas of hurt, injury, or pain. It's not just worldly wisdom expressed in the popular adage, "What doesn't kill you makes you stronger," but a pearl of wisdom gained from suffering and insight into what really matters to you. It is rather a few things in life are easy.

What is the process of recovering from a traumatic event that challenges a person's core beliefs which can make a person more resilient and sometimes even grateful for what they have received by allowing them to see the world more clearly after this traumatic experience? Assess the extent to which someone has achieved this growth after trauma. I can now clearly see growth, appreciation for life, new opportunities in life, personal strength, and most importantly spiritual change or renewal.

I think you might see how living through a life-threatening traumatic experience and coming out of the *other side* can affect these areas. The pain Paul experienced (mentioned in earlier passages) keeps our thoughts and actions focused on what really matters and lasts.

Many years later my trauma was used as a catalyst to be an advocate for others. The role a church or community can play in helping people amid painful and traumatic experiences is to give them hope that they too can experience a sense of growth because God redeemed even their suffering. The beauty of being Christian is that we are all part of a larger story, and we can walk through the toughest struggles together, offering camaraderie and making the journey bearable.

David, who I believe to be one of the most traumatized

people in the Bible, declared in Psalm 34:18, "The Lord is near to the brokenhearted He saves those who are broken in spirit [contrite in heart, sincerely repenting of their sins]."

Working through emotional trauma can be painful. But like physical recovery, emotional recovery requires short-term illness for long-term health and happiness. The willingness to work through trauma may seem obvious, but many people unconsciously hesitate. They may think they want freedom and liberty, but something inside is holding them to pain and hurt. Addressing deep-seated pain is not easy. In a way, it feels like reliving it all. But there is one thing you need to remember: Jesus is the healer. He took all your pain on the cross—physical and emotional—so that you could live a life of freedom. If you let Him heal your wounds, you'll live a life you never dreamed of.

If fear, anger, insecurity, or any other response to emotional trauma has been part of your life for a long period of time as you work to remove those harmful feelings and habits, you need to also fill the void. It isn't enough to just say, "I won't fear anymore." You must take two steps: (1) resist fear and (2) replace the spirit of fear with firm belief.

As you find your identity in Christ and develop your relationship with God, you will find that you drive away any signs of emotional trauma. When you start your life again with these ways to overcome emotional trauma, God will heal your wounds, and no one will doubt that you have had trouble in life because you will be filled with faith, hope, joy, peace, and love. You may have walked through the fire, but like Shadrach, Meshach, and Abednego, you won't even smell the smoke when you come out.

God is with us and in control of our suffering. It is during times of great pain and suffering that we often feel farthest from God. Where is he? Has he forgotten me? How can he allow it? The same is true of the lives of great men of biblical faith. Look at David (Psalm 13:1) "How long will it be, O Lord? Will you ever forget me?" From our finite human perspective, pain and suffering seem contrary to our imaginations. Through our trials and tribulations, we have a chance to get closer to God.

In James 1:2, we are told to "consider it nothing but joy" when we go through difficult times. I'm supposed to be happy when I'm in pain? Even Jesus was sad when he went through difficult times—at Lazarus's grave, in the garden of Gethsemane, and on the cross.

The third truth we are called to recognize is that through our trials and suffering, we have an opportunity to draw closer to God. In times of light, we often become self-reliant and forget that we need God. It is during difficult times when our faith is tested, such as death, imprisonment, and murder that we realize our need to depend entirely on Him.

James tells us that enduring hard times develops mature and perfect faith in James 1:4, "And let endurance have its perfect result and do a thorough work, so that you may be perfect and completely developed [in your faith], lacking in nothing." We are constantly being conformed to the image of Christ, and suffering is a necessary part of this transformation.

Jesus understood what it meant to suffer. We do not worship a distant, inaccessible god. We worship a God who knows what it means to be human, and He knows what it means to suffer. Hebrews 2:17–18 says, "Therefore, it was essential that He had to be made like His brothers [mankind] in every respect, so that He might [by experience] become a merciful and faithful High Priest in things related to God, to make atonement [propitiation] for the people's sins [thereby wiping away the sin, satisfying divine justice, and providing a way of reconciliation between God and mankind]. Because He Himself [in His humanity] has suffered in being tempted, He is able to help and provide immediate assistance to those who are being tempted and exposed to suffering."

Just think about Jesus's life for a moment. He didn't experience just one traumatic event during His time on

Earth. His whole life was full of suffering. The prophet Isaiah told of His suffering hundreds of years before His birth (Isaiah 53:3–5). He was born into unimaginable poverty in a country occupied by a cruel army. He narrowly escaped a mass slaughtering of children that was ordered because of His birth (Matthew 2:16). He was physically assaulted by Satan (Matthew 4:1–11), persecuted because of His teachings (Luke 4:28–29), thought insane by His family (Mark 3:21), betrayed by His own disciple (Mark 14:43–45), deserted by His friends, falsely arrested (Mark 14:56–59), publicly humiliated (Mark 15:16–20; Luke 23:8–12), beaten to the point of death (Matthew 27:26), and then slowly and painfully publicly executed by crucifixion as a common criminal (Matthew 27:33–39).

Well, if Jesus Christ can endure such pain and trauma and we are content with Him, God will continue to support us in our walk with Him. Next chapter, keep going!

CHAPTER 6

WAS THERE PURPOSE IN MY EMOTIONAL PAIN?

I t was in the agony that I was cornered, and I fell into the arms of Christ. When we are able to trust God more, we increase that sense of trust.

<u>Trust Begets Trust</u>

The more we choose to trust God, the more peace and joy we experience (Romans 15:13). God is pleased to give us the fruits of peace and joy, but it begins with trust. Even amid emotional pains from this world, we have the opportunity to give glory to God (John 9:3). Our wonderful God can turn ashes into beauty, sorrow into joy, and despair into praise (Isaiah 61:3). Through suffering, we become strong, steadfast, and determined (1 Peter 5:10).

Have you emerged from a heartbreaking season stronger than ever? You go into the season believing in Pee-Wee Herman and starting to believe in Superman. God works in your pain. Emotional pain prepares us to help others (2 Corinthians 1:3–4). Sharing God's faithfulness comforts others and brings God glory. It reminds the person you are comforting that they are not alone.

Pain changes you and your desires (Psalm 73:21–28). But when you get to the other side of the pain, you are different. How can you be the same? You are reminded of the brokenness around you and within you. I can no longer escape the pain. I had to stop fighting it. It's time to surrender; my pain has a purpose. My experiences have prompted me to reflect and make new life choices, deepening my compassion and empathy for others. I wake up to gratitude and have gratitude for all that I have. This pain drives me to act and face my emotions.

There is something therapeutic about telling my story. I had to gain self-esteem by expressing my pain and feelings. My story should not be put on hold. It should be told. Pain doesn't discredit me, but beauty and strength can be found in my brokenness. Finding meaning in your pain is an important part of healing. You may never understand *why* this pain occurs; in fact, the randomness of life can drive people mad. Decide how to live with your painful experience. It's natural to turn your head away when faced with painful events, especially if you feel overwhelmed. Sometimes in times of crisis, you have to deny the pain and embrace the isolation. Other times, it's important to face and acknowledge your pain. Denial can be adaptive and even helpful, but when you are at unhealthy levels, denying pain can lead to long-term health problems such as anxiety or panic attacks, depression, and trouble sleeping. Reaching out to God through journaling often helps me recover from trauma. Journaling is another practice we can incorporate into our lives to commune with God. You can write anything that comes to your mind. This can also be a form of mindfulness and can be a great way to get things out of your head and onto paper.

Some people prefer ad hoc journaling, and another form of writing that is often helpful in dealing with trauma is the healing letter. This is a letter you write but never send to anyone. It could be a letter to someone who has been traumatized, a letter to tell someone about a trauma you may never tell yourself, or a letter to your past or future self. Some people also use this method to write letters to God or write lamentations to God. You certainly don't have to do them all.

Most importantly, when you get to the other side of the emotional pain, you realize that it has brought glory to God because it has increased my faith and increased my trust in him. All of this makes me more capable of helping others. By helping others, God built a prison ministry that has helped thousands of incarcerated women of faith. Does my pain make sense? God has comforted us in our afflictions and has helped us. We tell you from our own experience how God comforts you tenderly when you go through the same affliction. He will give you the strength to endure. God wants you to use your pain to help others. Romans 5:3–5 says, "And not only this, but [with joy] let us exult in our sufferings and rejoice in our hardships, knowing that hardship [distress, pressure, trouble] produces patient endurance; and endurance, proven character [spiritual maturity]; and proven character, hope and confident assurance [of eternal salvation]. Such hope [in God's promises] never disappoints us, because God's love has been abundantly poured out within our hearts through the Holy Spirit who was given to us."

How do you surrender your pain to God? Whatever your situation is, you can start by praying in faith: "God, I know you have the power to change this." Then ask God for help. It is appropriate to say, "God, I ask for your help. I am in pain right now both emotionally and physically." God is able. While past pain has ruined your life, God says a breakthrough is imminent. Follow through and don't get discouraged or fail. This is a new day full of new opportunities and great potential. God is with you to give you a future and hope. Never doubt God's ability to move on and direct your path. Jeremiah 29:11 says, "For I know the plans and thoughts that I have for you,' says the Lord, 'plans for peace and well-being and not for disaster, to give you a future and a hope."

I refuse to be discouraged or hopeless. Despite the difficulties I faced, God gave me the strength to persevere and triumph. Focus on what works rather than what doesn't. If you ask for wisdom, God will give it without reservation. Have faith in Psalm 46:1 which says, "God is our refuge and strength [mighty and impenetrable], A very present and well-proved help in trouble." I realize that the past is in the past. I can't control what happened, but I can do a lot for the future. Set your heart and mind on doing whatever God has for you. God prepared the way.

Isaiah 40:4–5 says, "Every valley shall be raised, And every mountain and hill be made low; And let the rough ground become a plain, And the rugged places a broad valley. And the glory and majesty and splendor of the Lord will be revealed, And all humanity shall see it together; For the mouth of the Lord has spoken it." Never underestimate the power of God to heal. Believe without hesitation; trust God completely and never doubt for a moment. If you search with all your heart, you will find it. Please, it will be given. Do not be afraid! Matthew 7:7–11 says, "Ask and keep on asking and it will be given to you; seek and keep on seeking and you will find; knock and keep on knocking and the door will be opened to you. For everyone who keeps on asking receives, and he who keeps on seeking finds, and to him who keeps on knocking, it will be opened. Or what man is there among you who, if his son asks for bread, will [instead] give him a stone? Or if he asks for a fish, will [instead] give him a snake? If you then, evil [sinful by nature] as you are, know how to give good and advantageous gifts to your children, how much more will your Father who is in heaven [perfect as He is] give what is good and advantageous to those who keep on asking Him!"

The troubles don't seem to be over, but you have the mental advantage. Take your burdens to God in prayer, and He will give you wisdom and guidance to help you overcome them. God sees your plight, but there's nothing He can't handle when you trust Him to see you through. Psalm 18:2 says, "The Lord is my rock, my fortress, and the One who rescues me; My God, my rock and strength in whom I trust and take refuge; My shield, and the horn of my salvation, my high tower—my stronghold."

When you feel abandoned, alone, and without friends, God is your very present help in times of trouble. Come to God when you have been deserted and are desolate. Proverbs 18:24 says, "The man of too many friends [chosen indiscriminately] will be broken in pieces and come to ruin, But there is a [true, loving] friend who [is reliable and] sticks closer than a brother."

God closes an old chapter in my life, and He starts me over. This is not only a time for reflection but also for reviewing and planning for the next phase. There are some things God asks me to leave without regret. I have learned from my mistakes and enjoyed many victories in my walk with Christ. Isaiah 42:9 says, "Indeed, the former things have come to pass, Now I declare new things; Before they spring forth I proclaim them to you."

As God puts an end to many aspects of my life and circumstances, let the past get behind you before you start looking forward and moving forward. Use turning points and be sensitive to the leading of the Holy Spirit.

Philippians 3:13–14 says, "Brothers and sisters, I do not consider that I have made it my own yet; but one thing I do: forgetting what lies behind and reaching forward to what lies ahead, I press on toward the goal to win the [heavenly] prize of the upward call of God in Christ Jesus."

CHAPTER 7

THE OTHER SIDE OF THIS

To fully understand how God uses adverse situations to bring us to a place of peace, I've learned to be still. I've also learned through the trials and tribulations of life that He is all I've ever needed. He is all I've ever really had. Sometimes in life, circumstances may bring about interruptions. Many years ago I received the biggest interruption ever. My mother was diagnosed with stage 3 cancer and given eight months to live. At that very moment, my faith journey began, and it was tested and tried in every area of my life. After numerous sessions of chemotherapy, radiation, and prayers, my mother Thelma Lee Hunt-Davis was called home to be with the Lord in August 1994. Precisely five months after that, my brother was murdered! He was an innocent bystander whose life was cut short in his prime. He was also an inspiring hip-hop artist who had received notice the day before that he was being signed to a deal with Sony Music. He was my inspiration and the *big brother* that everyone would want to have. After this tragedy, who could have envisioned what happened next? I received a call from the VA hospital exactly two days after the death of my brother while someone stated, "I know that your family has gone through a very difficult time. However, I have to bring you the bad news that your father, who was stable just this morning, has suddenly passed away." I was devastated but I knew that God's hands had to be on me because how could one individual have the capacity to remain steadfast amid these traumatic events and still manage to display strength, stability, and faith while seeking a career at the same time?

It was hard for me to believe that in just five months I had lost three immediate family members that I cherished so dearly. I realized there had to be something *on the other side of this*. Sometimes it would seem as if the broken pieces in my life were never going to be back together again. But I learned that as I kept on developing my faith in the living God, I could rise. Sure, it took time for me to shake myself loose, but I had to look over all of what I was going through to resolve and allow God to heal, restore, and fix it. I had to get out of my way and allow God to take control so that I could heal and be prepared on the off chance that there were any future trials.

I said *future trials* because I discovered that my trials were not yet over. In July 1999, my sixteen-year-old stepson was unjustly shot and killed. He was a star football player in high school. This new tragedy devastated our family, especially my other two sons and my husband. Trust me when I say that it was only because of my experience of being steadfast in the prior circumstances that allowed me to hold it together. I leaned on my faith and just knew that there had to be something on the other side of this. Previously, my husband was there to comfort me, yet even amid my agony, I had to comfort and console my husband. I also had to console the boys' grief that they were going through. I had to handle this and that *mothering* had to quickly rise to an altogether different level because of this catastrophe. How can you even speak when tragedy hits you by surprise and makes you speechless? It was only because of my faith that I was able to survive.

After many years of healing, my husband and I decided to purchase a house for our family. The other side of this began to manifest itself in my life. We got the house with limited finances and an unfavorable credit score. My husband said that he had heard from God and that all we needed to do to get our hands on the property was to claim it and it would be ours. Within seven months, we closed the deal on a beautiful four-bedroom house with a five-car driveway. It became the place where we all began to rebuild our lives and reestablish our goals. My husband began to build his own accounting business called Esor Accounting Services which proved to be very rewarding. His company would assist nonprofit organizations throughout New York City with their financial reporting. Our family was working together in faith to build our ministry as well as our business all while keeping God at the forefront of our endeavors. We received God's favor and started ministering together at the county jail on weekends. We saw that we needed to give back to others what had been so freely given to us. Before long, my husband and I became pastors of Upon This Rock Ministries Inc. Our vision was and still is to see the salvation of those who have been lost in our inner-city neighborhoods. We would like to see their minds renewed by the power of God not only by assisting in their spiritual growth but also by interacting with our community in a way to remediate the social and educational problems that challenge the neighborhoods that we have been called to serve. Working in the inner city, where the economic, educational, and health issues are in large numbers, is our obsession and desire. We very quickly became a resource center for the underprivileged. People began to flock toward our calling. After several years of growing a successful ministry and rising to community prominence, we experienced a major political, religious, and legal setback as scandal and false allegations came against my husband. The residual effect of this scandal caused our family to lose a large portion of our six-figure annual income. My husband was wrongly convicted and subsequently imprisoned for two years. However, God has always provided for us. My husband, being a servant of God and highly educated, was able to write his appeal to the Supreme Court and was released early by decision. He also became the first inmate of the facility in which he was imprisoned to pastor to the entire inmate population! It was then that I knew that there definitely was something on *the other side of this*!

The many challenges in my life helped me to discover who I was, and just when I thought they were over, more showed up. One morning around 10:00 a.m., I received documents from a bank regarding my home. The one thing I did not need at that moment was a lawsuit. It wasn't a lawsuit this time, but due to the loss of income, my home had gone into foreclosure. Right then and there, my feelings were so feeble. Because my husband was not present, I didn't know where I would go. I began to pray. Being a prayer warrior, I had always sought the Lord first. The Lord began to speak to me and announced that I would survive this battle despite it feeling as if I was under an insurmountable opposition. But I still had faith!

As I looked into the summons and complaint against me, I started to ask the Lord, "What should I do?" Having a background in business was not what I needed at that moment. What I needed was a lawyer. God began to reassure me that everything would turn out fine. It was so risky yet at the same time I moved within a surety that God was my advocate as I was reminded of a scripture, Isaiah 10:27, "So it will be in that day, that the burden of the Assyrian will be removed from your shoulders and his yoke from your neck. The yoke will be broken because of the fat." A promise of God may be delayed, but His Word tells us it is not denied.

I was reminded of yet another biblical account regarding the prophet Daniel and the delay he experienced in the manifestation of his request to God. Daniel 10:1–12 says that Daniel was a man of boldness. He was not hesitant to ask and trust God notwithstanding when it was unlawful for him to do so. When I was faced with foreclosure, I felt a sense of shame. I also felt as if I was a failure. I was worried about the negative effect that this would have on my FICO score. I knew that these types of things could affect any future real estate purchases and even the ability to rent an apartment. Like many people being faced with foreclosure, I felt helpless. In any case, I still believed that there was something special waiting for me on *the other side of this*!

Once I understood the foreclosure process, I discovered that there were practical strategies that anyone could utilize to save their home. God gave me through His favor a godsent individual and a crash course to gain the knowledge and direction I needed. Again my faith was activated! Little did I know that a business was in the making. As I began to share and educate others about challenging the banks about ownership of their property and how important it was to respond to any complaint within twenty to thirty days, DDR Consultants came into being. DDR Consultants is now a multiservice center that provides a variety of services to residents in Westchester, Putnam, and Nassau counties as well as the five boroughs of New York City. DDR Consultants was birthed out of my own personal experience. We focus on getting the best possible results for those in need. Our mission is to educate those who want to learn more about the foreclosure process, which has become an epidemic in our nation. We also assist families facing foreclosure by helping them to find alternatives through research and documentation. So many homeowners have been affected by predatory and abusive subprime mortgage lending practices. While DDR specialists are not lawyers, we make sure that families know their rights, and we guide them to the appropriate legal counsel in New York State. DDR Consultants has become my *other side of this*. We have been blessed with a 100 percent success rate for our clients. We have kept them in their homes! I am so pleased with the smiles I see on our clients' faces because of the work that we have performed.

My past has made my present more powerful! Not only has our business placed me on the other side of this, but the same has been true for Upon This Rock Ministries Inc., a faith-based 501(c)(3) organization. Within this company, we created a program called the Family Restoration Project of the Lower Hudson Valley Sub-Region (Westchester, Putnam, and Rockland counties). It is a collaborative initiative to help support the successful and safe transition of young fathers from detention, out-of-home placement, or incarceration to their families and communities. With other key partners, we are working to give a thorough project for lessening recidivism, advancing public safety, and enhancing results for young fathers coming back from detainment and veterans returning from tours of service, or incarceration, to reconnect with their families and communities.

I've learned that we should never let our circumstances cause us to lose hope. While trials and tribulations are often beyond our control, our behavior and how we respond to these trials mean everything. During my trials, I never lost sight of my dreams and aspirations. I didn't allow my situation or people to break me. My victory might have been delayed, but it wasn't denied. Under the weight of intense adversity, I learned to understand that what we call *pain*, God has called it *preparation*! When you have faith and hold on, you can get to the other side of this!

Printed in the United States
by Baker & Taylor Publisher Services